G000241992

he used to be me

he used to be me

ANNE WALSH Donnelly

NEW ISLAND

HE USED TO BE ME
First published in 2024 by
New Island Books
Glenshesk House, 10 Richview Office Park
Clonskeagh, Dublin D14 V8C4
Republic of Ireland
www.newisland.ie

Print ISBN: 978-1-84840-907-1
eBook ISBN: 978-1-84840-908-8

British Library Cataloguing in Publication Data. A CIP catalogue
record for this book is available from the British Library.

Set in 11 on 16pt Brunel Text
Typeset by New Island
Edited by Amanda Bell
Cover design by Jack Smyth, jacksmyth.co
Claw illustration by Kathryn Slattery
This advance review copy printed by Sprint Print, Dublin

New Island received financial assistance from The Arts Council (An
Chomhairle Ealaíon), Dublin, Ireland.

New Island Books is a member of Publishing Ireland.

10 9 8 7 6 5 4 3 2 1

For Brian and Hannah

Contents

I SIT ON THE STONE that will mark the bed of my bones. You'll find the used-to-be-me, soon, flat body, washed up, wrinkly skin. No silly grin. You'll say what a waste of a life. Tut-tut sounds jump out. Dangle like worms from your crow's mouth.

You'll make my letters M A T T – sound of steel on granite, tap, tap, with your chisel.

What about D A F T?

You'll conveniently forget and say, 'We were never that cruel, surely?'

And what about the M A T T H E W you never knew?

After a few prayers, you'll slurp your stout.

Breathe out.

'God rest his soul.'

Me?

I'll jump on a white horse and fly to *Tír na nÓg*.

Now

You call me Daft Matt. *Daft old man.* Say I've no face. You must think I've no ears either. I feel your eyes on me, staring at the crown of my head, lice playing hopscotch on my scalp and hump on my shoulders as big as Nephin mountain. I'm not as mad as you think. I've good reason for looking at the ground. I haven't forgotten how to look up. I'm searching for the claws of the *cága*. Ones you call Devil's feet. I've holes in my soles from walking the town. Even the claws on the shoe-maker's shop are gone. They've leapt off the walls, to escape your grimy gunk and big bulldozers. Claws jump off Castlebar walls race hell skell through grey streets

unseen,

unheard,

untouched,

odourless,

vapourless,

senseless.

I'm standing on the white line in the middle of Main Street. Turning my head this way and that. Car horns blow, their bumpers with faces like castrated bulls. There's a smell of dead *cág* rising from manholes. Have they drowned in the sewers? I hold my nose and jump from street to pavement, look at the cracks. Steam rises. Ghosty frosty breaths. You guffaw in my ears. Stop taunting me. I'm not daft. I just want my *cága* claws back. No, no, they're not Devil's feet. Nobody wants to see a Devil's foot.

I USED TO THINK those claws were the only things that kept me above sea-level.

OUCH! THEY'VE COME BACK. They pinch my ears, pull my hair, collar of my jacket, leg of my trousers. STOP. Don't pull my laces, I'll trip.

> *Let's go to the lake, Matt.*

Let's go to my farm.

> *You don't live there anymore.*

Over the mountains, past the fjord so deep if I dived in, I'd end up bumping into the wicked god they call Balor and he'd stare at me with his evil eye and I'd never surface again.

> *That's the wrong way.*

But if I climbed the highest peak, I'd be able to touch the cloud Eoin Paul is sitting on and if I played with the sheep clinging to the steep slopes they'd baa at me, they wouldn't call me daft, we would just

> *plaaay plaaay all daaay long.*

I SHOO AWAY THE sheep in my brain and run to the edge of town. Then I sit on a stone wall and if I looked up, I'd see the mountains that stand between me and my farm.

They have all sorts of blotchy patches on their faces. Some are purple-green, some bushy-brown, some the colour of calf-scour. And there's strips of gunky green that remind me of the lino in St Mary's. There's a wood of pines on the far side full of Christmas trees that look like the carpet in Mr T's office and might be as soft.

Aren't some humans awful cruel though? Not only calling me daft but killing all those trees just to have one in their sitting room that they can put lights and shiny balls on and an angel on top. I wonder what angels think of humans killing trees and putting statues of them on top. The church bell rings. Six times. It tells me it's time for tea.

> *But, you're not hungry, Matt.*
> *Níl ocras ort.*

Time to go back to the house I'm supposed to call home.

THE *CÁGA* HAVE QUIETENED, church bells stop them from digging into my hump and they scurry away. I'm not hungry for tea so I go to the lake. I sit on a bench, feel the cold and damp seep into the bones of my bum. I open my lips wide and out come all these words, they

      float
                  in
                                  the
          air.

I want to tell my story. I'm not much good at writing so all I can do is let the words out and hope they land on someone else and that person will grab the tumble jungle of letters and words and make them into proper sentences. Someone who has special antennae on their head that grab a's, b's, c's and d's as they go from head

to arms
          to hands
                    to fingers
                            to pen
                                    to page.

Sometimes my words come out the way Goldilocks would like them – Just Right. I have to work really hard though. Usually when I'm with Mr T in his hospital office or talking to my daughter on the phone and I know if I saw Harriet again they would be – Just Right.

Only thing is, that would be a waste of time 'cos now she's the one with the

> tumble
>
> > jungle
> >
> > > words.

> > > > *She'll never be.*
> > > > *Just Right.*

We had a see-saw marriage in a jigsaw life. When one of us was up, the other was down ...

> > > > *Suas agus síos.*

... and after the fall all the pieces of our life got scattered and some were lost and you can't have a proper jigsaw if some of the pieces are missing.

> > > > *Briste.*

Then

WILL I TELL YOU about the Matt-hew you never knew?

Half-wit, Daddy used to call me. Mammy said it was 'cos the whiskey pickled his tongue and made his words all vinegary. I used to wonder what made his arms go wild when he'd wallop me with a hawthorn stick after I'd go rambling and forget to close the gate and the cattle'd go walkabout. Mammy'd go hunting for me. He'd go hunting for them. She'd find me dangling from a branch of the oak tree in the middle of the top field, making monkey sounds. I wanted to go live in a jungle, have a gorilla for a Daddy, 'cos they'd surely be kinder than him.

Evenings, when Daddy was in the pub and I'd be jumping on my bed, pretending to be an angel bouncing in the clouds with Eoin Paul. Mammy'd bring me downstairs and make me a mug of hot milk. We'd snuggle by the fire and listen to the new radio she bought out of the money Granddad left her when he died. One night, it was Halloween and the man on the radio was talking about witches on broomsticks flying across the moon and I asked Mammy if the witches would find Eoin Paul and bring him home so I could be whole again. She looked out the kitchen window at the black sky and said in a baby goat's voice, 'You're perfect, the way you are.'

What about the half that should have lived, Daddy'd bellow when his stomach was full of stout. The day I turned eighteen was the last time Daddy called me half-wit. I grabbed his shotgun from the top of the dresser, pointed it at him, my hands all sweaty and shaky. The rashers on the frying pan hissed and burnt, sent smelly smoke to the rafters and made me sneeze. Mammy skittered around the kitchen like a chicken escaping a butcher's knife. Her squawking made me drop the gun to the flagstones. Daddy roared, 'It's time for him to go.'

'No,' Mammy said. 'Over. My. Dead. Body.'

WHEN I WAS SMALL and did silly things, like make chocolate cakes with cow pats, Mammy used to say, 'That's daft, Matt.'

Her 'daft' sounded like a lamb's bleat and felt like a sheepskin rug. No hint of a knife. Or glint of a blade.

One day, there was no Mammy to say swallowing worms was daft. All I could say when they covered her with earth was, 'That's daft.' And what's even more daft is I've forgotten how to hug 'cos

Dead
Arms
Fools
Touch.

WHEN EOIN PAUL AND ME were seven we pretended to be warriors from the Fianna. I was Fionn Mac Cumhaill and he was Oisín.

Glaine ár gcroí.

We'd make spears out of ash sticks and chase pretend boars around the yard and shout at the top of our voices.

Neart ár ngéag.

We made a secret pact that we would never get old and contrary like Daddy. We would stay young forever. Or do like Oisín, jump on a white mare and fly to ...

Tír na nÓg.

EOIN PAUL AND ME were ten when the world ignited, turned into a comet and smashed into the ground. We were burning up so badly.

'Like two balls of fire,' Mammy said. 'Not even all the ice in the North Pole will cool ye down, ye have to go to hospital.'

We cried and cried when Mammy hugged us goodbye and she cried and cried and Daddy ...

He went to the pub.

... I can't rightly remember what he did or said.

'Don't worry,' the doctor said, 'they'll be right in no time.'

Can't trust them doctors.

ONE DAY, AFTER forty days, two strangers walked up the smelly corridor of the hospital, the woman in a green flowery dress and the man wearing a black Mass coat and a hat like John Wayne's.

'You have to go home with them, all the red bumps on your skin have gone to heaven with Eoin Paul,' said Nurse.

I jumped up and down in her office and said, 'That's not fair, I want to go to heaven too.'

She said the two strangers were my Mammy and Daddy but I didn't believe her. I just wanted to stay in the ward with the other children and eat the ice-cream Nurse gave me. But that was a secret and I wasn't supposed to tell anyone. She'd get into trouble with the matron if she knew she was giving me ice-cream at two in the morning.

The woman that was supposed to be my Mammy bent down and whispered that I wasn't to be afraid and that she'd buy me a bullseye on the way home. I thought, if she was able to read my mind, then she must be my Mammy. The man in the John Wayne hat didn't say anything.

WHEN I CAME OUT of hospital, Eoin Paul came too only he was in a wooden box and the woman that was supposed to be my Mammy turned into a weeping birch, the man that was supposed to be my Daddy was really a tall pine. Me, a cross-bred sapling, or as the bucks in school called me, a mongrel tree. I dreamt of stealing Farmer Joe's chainsaw, to cut through Daddy's trunk so he'd know how it felt, to be knocked to the ground. I imagined the fun I'd have stamping each and every one of his cones into the muck. Mammy's birch would stop weeping, her branches would reach towards the sky, and it would never hailstone in our back yard again.

AFTER EOIN PAUL died, everything else did too. The runt of a lamb that we had in the tea-chest beside the fire since Easter Sunday died the night Eoin Paul lay in a wooden box in the parlour. We used to fight over who would feed him before he got sick. I wished I had someone to fight with again.

Miss Piggy rolled over in the sty in her sleep and killed three of her bonhams. Blight turned the potatoes to mush. The apples in the orchard fell off the trees in July, Mulligan's goats broke in. They gobbled all the crabs before me and Mammy could rescue them.

The milk in the churns turned sour overnight. Mammy said it was Daddy's fault for staying in the pub for so long. Daddy said it was Mammy's nagging that was the cause.

A stone in the top field broke the blade of the hay mower. Daddy threw a sod of turf at me. I was supposed to have picked up all the stones and thrown them in the ditch. I wanted to throw a sod of turf at myself, but I was too near my own body to do any great damage.

I ran to the old quarry, stood on a big rock, stared into the black water that smelt of green diesel. And

I wondered if I jumped in, would everything else stop dying. I lifted one foot, leaned forward and whispered, 'Hello Eoin Paul. Goodbye Mammy.'

Then I felt something grab my jumper. It pulled me so hard I fell back and landed on my bum. And it cawed.

Maaw   Maaw   Maaw

And it told me that one son was enough for any Mammy to lose.

THE NEXT NIGHT I had my best dream ever. It was so good, I didn't want to wake up. I wanted to go back deep into sleep, deep into the dream. Eoin Paul and me, alive, free, jumping like billy goats in the lower field, scaring the birds with our fox's laughs.

But the morning sun grabbed a slash hook and sliced through my dreams. I rubbed my eyes, prayed to Holy God, held my breath, pegged my nose with one hand, covered my mouth with the other. My cheeks puffed out. The cock crowed outside my bedroom window. My hands were not strong enough to keep the air out of my body. Me wanting to play with Eoin Paul was no match for the nose that wanted to breathe. I exploded like a puffball into a mess of snot and tears.

'Sorry Eoin Paul, God won't let me be with you.'

Eoin Paul dies.
Big boys don't cry.
Eoin Paul dies.
Big boys don't cry.
Eoin Paul dies.
What do I do with the water in my eyes?
Drip. Drop. Drip.
Drop.
Big boys don't cry.
Even when brothers die.

PLAYING CAN HURT when you've no one to play with only yourself. Playing can hurt when your Daddy wants a whole boy not a half-a-boy that can't milk a cow without spilling their milk all over the place. Playing can hurt when your Mammy calls you Eoin Paul.

Buachaillín bán.

And Eoin Paul doesn't answer and she cries and you cry 'cos you can't be him. You can only be you and she says there's only one of you and she loves you, only sometimes she forgets herself and I promise I'll never forget myself or herself or Eoin Paul's self and she cries again.

And before Daddy comes in for his dinner, we pick up all the tears real quick and hide them in the tea-chest beside the fire before he sees them and all hell breaks loose and it gives him a reason to grab the birch rod lying on top of the dresser so he can 'bate all the tears out of me' as he often says he will 'cos big boys don't cry even when brothers die.

THE DAY AFTER I watched Eoin Paul's coffin being lowered into the ground I sneaked out of my bedroom window in the middle of the night. I ran to the wild wood, a triangle of trees that stood in a corner of the top field. I fought my way through brambles and briars until I reached the tiny clearing in the centre. I scraped at the earth, sodden from a week of rain. When I had a hole big enough for my body to lie in, I gathered twigs and sticks to cover myself with and lay down. I slept and slept dreaming of the hedgehogs who would join me in October. I dreamt of waking in March, breaking free of my bones, going home and finding Eoin Paul asleep in his bed. Johnny No Nose found me the next morning, lifted me out of the hole, carried me to his wagon which was full of old pots and pans, and his missus gave me goodie for breakfast and it was the creamiest of milk and the sweetest of bread I'd ever tasted. Then Johnny No Nose brought me home and Daddy gave him a sack of potatoes for his troubles.

I WISH GOD WAS a woman 'cos I know a She God
would never be so cruel as to take a brother
from a boy or a son from a mother.
Only a He God would do such a thing.

CLOUDS ARE JUST like humans, they never stay still for long, always moving, moving, moving across the sky, changing into all sorts of shapes and colours, one minute they look like blobs of melted ice-cream, the next – clumps of tadpole spawn and the next – lumps of black coal. You never know where you stand with them, it's not a good idea to be friends with patches in the sky, can't trust them.

You can trust us, Matt.

Only thing is – Eoin Paul is sleeping on one of those clouds and I don't know which one.

He's in Tír na nÓg, Matt.

EVERY DAY AFTER Eoin Paul died I used to walk around and around the farm yard, looking at the sky, searching for his cloud until one Sunday after Mass, Mammy said, 'If you keep looking up and the wind changes, your head will stay that way.'

'Sorry, Mammy, will I go and mulch some mangels for the pigs?'

The next day I fell and split my lip and Daddy said, 'If you don't keep your head down, I'll make it stay down.'

So I stopped looking at the sky. And that's when my hump came up.

The only day I look up now is on Eoin Paul's birthday.

THE CHRISTMAS AFTER I turned eighteen, Mammy gave, or maybe it was God who gave me a present worse than a lump of coal. On St Stephen's night, I found her crying in her bedroom. I thought it was on account of Daddy being in the pub since breakfast but she shook her head and said, 'I wish that was all that was upsetting me.'

She put my hand on her tummy and I could feel a lump as big and as hard as a sliotar.

'I have to go to hospital in January, I'm afraid I might not come out of it again.'

'Then don't go,' I bawled.

'Matt, you're getting too old for tears. Now listen to me, if I don't come out again, go to the old milk churn in the hayshed and take the manure bag at the bottom of it and leave and don't come back.'

I hopped into bed beside her and hugged her so tight tears rolled from her cheek onto mine. That was the last time we cried.

THE DAY AFTER we buried Mammy, I went down to the hay shed, took the manure bag from the milk churn. I looked out at the three-acre field and the hay that had yet to be saved. Breeze, our old donkey, brayed from the paddock. I went over to the gate and patted his head.

'Sorry, Breeze,' I said. 'I have to go walkabout, like those lads in Australia do.'

He shook his head as if to say, no, no, no. But the *cága* said,

> *Time to go, Matt,*
> *go, go, go.*

I left the *cága* behind, to guard Eoin Paul and Mammy's graves.

> *No, no, no.*

After Then Before Now

IN KATHMANDU A body smouldered on a stone slab beside a smelly river. A man that said he was a monk kept going on about being born again and having a different body. And according to him you could end up being a cow or a sow or even a midge. And he was giving me an awful headache.

So I went off to climb a mountain 'cos those mountains in Nepal are the nearest thing to heaven on earth. But what he said got me wondering.

We're not Eoin Paul or Mammy,
we're past, present and future you.

HARRIET AND ME met in Singapore.

We warned you, we did.

She walked as if the man above was pulling her head with an invisible rope towards the clouds, her hair blood-orange like the feathers on a bantam hen, and she brought me on a tour of Little India and Chinatown.

'Tis far from China that you were reared.

And in a market we sat on concrete stools sipping stout, gazing at each other. Smells that she said were coriander, ginger and garlic filling our noses and there were men talking in a funny language all around us.

Crack!

At a Korean food stall a knife severed the head of a cock. Its body shook as if it was having a fit. We watched until it went limp. The sticky heat made me want to scratch my groin. I rubbed sweat from my brow while the cock's blood dripped from the counter onto the concrete floor. Harriet grasped my hand and laughed like a hen clucking but there was no sound of *cága* cawing. And Harriet's cluck put a spell on me in a way cawing never would.

WE MARRIED IN UBUD, a little village in the middle of Bali.

Duub, duup, duup.

Silly *cága*, that's not a word.

Harriet wore a white silk dress she had made in a tailor shop in Bangkok. I can't remember what I wore. We had banana pancakes for breakfast. And we asked a Bali buck who said he was a Hindu priest to marry us. He said some peculiar words neither of us really understood and then we said, 'We do.'

You didn't.

And that was it, done and dusted in five minutes. No Mass to have to sit through. Afterwards we ate vegetable curry off big green leaves and danced on the beach all night long. And the local lads thought we were mad. But we didn't care. And Harriet wore pink and purple flowers in her hair. And we had sex all night in our hut. And back in Mayo, the very same night, Daddy's heart stopped.

Hip, hip, hurrah.
There was no sound of a bean sí ag caoineadh.

WE NEVER LIKED HER. We didn't.
But would Matt listen? No.
It was she that put all the geiseanna on him.
He was doomed from the start.
He couldn't eat peas with potatoes.
He couldn't wear socks the same colour as his jocks.
He couldn't go to Mass every ninth Sunday.
He couldn't sleep in a bed
the third Wednesday of every month.
He couldn't kill a wriggly worm.
He couldn't leave any house after midnight.
He couldn't get out of bed every second Tuesday
if a cock didn't crow.
He was doomed from the start.
And once he broke a geis there was no going back.

I FOUND OUT ABOUT Daddy's heart stopping when I opened my PO Box in Darwin. If Harriet hadn't convinced me to send him a postcard saying we got married in Bali, they might never have tracked me down.

When I told Harriet, she said, 'We have to go back.'

'What about the life we'd planned in Sydney?'

'There's a farm at home, waiting for you and me and the children we'll have together.'

I cut my hair, stopped wearing my baggy paisley trousers.

They made you look like an amadán.

Gave my leather poncho to a charity shop. Harriet stopped wearing henna and flowers in her hair. We turned from hippies into normal country folk. The jigsaw of our life started to take shape. All the pieces that didn't fit, we threw away.

Hey, you can't throw us away.

All the pieces that stayed seemed perfect. But the thing with jigsaws is, unless you Super Glue the pieces together, one little tip and they can all fall apart again. And priests and horses are the two most dangerous things to have near a jigsaw that's not Super Glued.

WILL I TELL YOU how the Windy Gap got its name? Well, there was a stack of mountains that ran from one end of the county to the other, a big black stack, and one day God was chasing the Devil around Ireland but the Devil was too fast for God and God got tired running after him so He stopped. Then He took a deep breath up through his nose and blew and blew as hard as He could. The Devil scrambled over the Mayo mountains and God's breath was so fast and furious it blew a big hole in them.

Harriet laughed as the train pulled into Castlebar and said, 'God, Matt, you've a dangerous imagination.'

> *That's a great story, Matt.*
> *We love it. More, more, more.*

I waved at the only taxi man at the station and we hopped into his purple Ford Escort.

'Take us home to the Windy Gap,' I said, and off we went.

MY SON WAS THREE, my daughter four, they helped Harriet make me a cake while I was out milking the cows and feeding the pigs. It was the lightest, softest sponge Harriet ever made and they put Smarties on top and the children wanted to put thirty candles on it but Harriet said three was enough and I blew out the candles, and they sang Happy Birthday and it was the best birthday ever.

Lá breithe shona duit.

THE LAST TIME I sang Happy Birthday to my son was when he turned five and it should have been his best birthday ever only that Harriet had bought him a new pair of black leather shoes and they were as shiny as a lump of Polish coal but a pair of shoes is not exactly what a boy of five wants for his birthday. But she said he needed a proper pair for Mass.

So I made him a spear out of a branch of an ash tree just like the ones me and Eoin Paul used to have when we were young and then Harriet got cross because I shouldn't be encouraging my son to go killing things. But that wasn't the case at all. And then her nagging got even worse on account of me saying I was going to bring him to the bog, 'cos I'd promised him the summer before that I'd bring him to the bog when he was five.

So when Harriet went to the village to get the shopping, I kept my promise. Only thing was, he was five in November and November's not really the best time to be going to the bog. He had a great time though, jumping off the turf banks into the water as black as his new shoes. But he got rightly soaked, he did.

Then on the way home we found a load of steel-grey feathers in the hawthorn bush beside the paddock.

And he wanted me to make an Indian band for his head like the ones he'd seen on the bucks in my western comic books. But when we landed into the kitchen with him mucked up to the eyeballs and me carrying a bunch of dirty feathers, well, Harriet got as cross as a goose when you'd go near her goslings.

And I wondered had someone kidnapped the woman I married.

It wasn't us, Matt.

BUT THEN HARRIET's favourite song came on the radio. Dana singing 'All kinds of everything remind me of you,' put a halt to her giving out for a minute.

I gave my son the bunch of feathers, wiped my hands on the arse of my trousers, waltzed towards Harriet and the lines criss-crossing her forehead got lighter until you could hardly see them at all and she let me take her in my arms and we danced around the kitchen and my son and daughter laughed and squealed.

While she was making the dinner, I gave my son a bath, and once the dinner was over I put himself and his sister to bed. And then I made Harriet a nice mug of strong tea with two spoons of sugar, just the way she likes it, and I snuggled up to her on the couch where she was reading her Woman's Way magazine. I said I was sorry about the bog and the feathers only I didn't think. She put down her magazine, turned to me and said, 'Oh Matt, you'll be the death of me yet.'

AND THEN WHO arrived at the door, only the young buck that was just out of the seminary a few months, wearing one of those bat-wing cassocks that priests wore in those days and his hair full of that Brylcreem stuff the Teddy Boys loved.

And Harriet jumped off the couch, tore off her apron and said, 'You'll have a cup of tea, Father.'

And he said, 'Ah, don't be going to any trouble but if you're making one for yourself I won't say no. I was just up at Flanaghan's giving poor Mary the last rites and seen as I was passing I thought I'd drop in to say hello.'

And I was thinking to myself that he seems to be passing our house an awful lot lately but I didn't say anything. Not that I could get a word in edgeways 'cos they were chatting away like two chirping chickens …

He knows no better   gone to the dogs
        Lord bless us and save us

and the wind would cut ya in two   it would surely
        promised snow tomorrow

made awful rain last night
        You do say a lovely Mass, Father

You do make a lovely cup of **tea**, Harriet

Too fond of the drink, he is
        I hear the poor wife has taken to the bed

        poor créatúr

That buck has fierce notions
           he didn't take it from the dresser

… you'd swear I wasn't in the room at all. And an awful blast of cold air had come into the kitchen with the priest. So I went out to the shed to get more turf for the fire. And then I sat on the wooden bench outside the back door and a hymn came into my head …

Silent night, holy night
All is calm, and all is bright

… and I don't know why 'cos Christmas was a whole month away and it was anything but a silent night.

Breeze III was braying like mad in the paddock, the cattle were bellowing in the cow house and Grey the new mare I'd bought in the Ballinasloe Horse Fair was snorting her head off in the stable.

IT WAS A SUNDAY morning and the children were fast asleep. Harriet and me lay in bed, just after I'd made love to her and I knew she enjoyed it 'cos she meowed exactly like our cat did after she'd had some cow's milk. And for five minutes, I felt like the king of my house.

Ard-Rí of your house.
Aaw, Aaw, Aaw.

'Maybe we could skip Mass just for one Sunday,' I said.

I didn't say that I couldn't stand the way the priest looked at her dress every Sunday and I couldn't stand the way she looked at him. I didn't tell her about the pounding in my head that made me dizzy when he preached about love being kind and patient, about love not being jealous, about love being trusting, about love not being angry.

She threw the covers off the bed. A blast of cold air made my willy stand to attention. She jumped out, pulled the wardrobe doors wide open, scrambled through her clothes looking for her best Sunday dress and couldn't find it.

After breakfast, she stood in the hallway, looking at the mirror, fixing her new hair-do, her Mass coat covering her house dress, and muttered, 'Where the hell is my good dress? I hope I don't faint at Mass from the heat.'

I couldn't tell her she'd never find that blasted dress. No, I couldn't tell her the slurry had gobbled it up. I knew once the words were out, they could never be put back in again.

And once the pieces of the jigsaw started to shift nothing would ever be the same.

Shame, shame, shame.

INSTEAD I TOLD her I had an awful headache and wasn't fit for Mass. And that the fence in the three-corner field needed fixing. As soon as the car left the yard, herself driving and my son and daughter standing on the seat waving out the back window, I ran to the stable, jumped onto Grey, forgot about the saddle. We galloped and galloped over thorny hedges, mucky dykes and stony fields. But I didn't notice any of it and I'm sure there were *cága* cawing and maybe even a claw pulling Grey's mane, trying to slow her down. But there was so much going on in my head and the picture of Harriet and the way she might be looking at the priest and the way he might be looking at her when he was preaching his sermon. There was nothing else I could see or hear or feel. And then I got to thinking of those that I loved the most in the world:

Eoin Paul
Mammy
Harriet
Son
Daughter.

You love us too, Matt.

And two out of five were gone. And maybe soon that might be five out of five. And maybe soon Harriet and the priest might run away and take my two little ones with them.

ONE DAY, MATT sat on a horse. The horse bucked. Matt flew through the air. Thump. Hump. Hit his head on a great rock. The hospital doctors couldn't put Matt's brains back together again.

Matt's wife couldn't look at him ever again. Matt dribbled and spewed like a colicky baby. In his fields, cows lowed, sheep bleated, horses neighed. In his farmyard, hens clucked, geese cackled, turkeys gobbled. In his house, cat meowed, toddlers giggled, radio sang ...

Top of the world, lookin' down on creation.

Every single living thing did exactly what they were supposed to do.

Except Matt.

'HE'LL BE RIGHT in no time,' said the chief doctor.

Manglam.

He was surrounded by a ring of young doctors, their shadows like those skyscrapers they have in New York, blocking the sun and chilling my bones. He handed a pile of pills to Harriet.

'You can take him home tomorrow. Make sure he takes two of these three times a day.'

I was still in my pyjamas when she came the next morning. My body felt as heavy as two bags of coal and I could hardly lift my arms. I couldn't even open my mouth to say hello.

'You're awful quiet today, Matt,' she said as she pulled up my trousers. I nodded.

Tap, tap, tap.

I jerked my head, looked out the window and saw a bunch of *cága.* I'd never seen them before.

'I still can't understand how you fell off the mare, you're such a good jockey,' she said.

It was the priest's fault.

'No more priest,' I said.

She stood back from me and said, 'Now you're making no sense.'

> *She loves the priest more than you, Matt.*
> *Haw, haw, haw.*

I stared at her, dug my nails into the palms of my hands. I could feel sweat race down the hollow of my back and the *cága* were making an awful racket. And they had my head moithered.

> *Caaw, caaw, caaw.*

They kept rapping on the windowpane. Louder than a shower of hailstones it was.

Then SMASH.

Bits of glass flew everywhere, one hit Harriet's brow, and a stream of blood gushed down her cheek onto the floor. She screamed and two nurses came running. That's all I remember. When I woke up, there was a tumble jungle of words floating in the air and I kept my eyes shut real tight.

'I can't have him at home. There's the farm to be looked after and two young children. He'd be too much to handle.'

> *Too much to handle.*

'You have to go,' she said, when I opened my eyes. 'You have to go to another hospital, just for a small while until you're fully better.'

She promised she'd visit, blathered on about the children and the lambing sheep. But all I could hear were the words ...

She doesn't love you anymore.

I remember once I told her that her breasts would never be too much for me to handle. She complained they were too big when she was pregnant. I loved the size of them in my hands and the way her nipples stiffened when my fingers played with them, before I dived into her plunge pool.

'Aren't you awful fancy,' she'd say, 'calling my thing that?'

I'd read about plunge pools in a *National Geographic*. I wasn't always stupid, you know.

Lying in the hospital bed, all I wanted was for her to jump in beside me, hold my face in her hands and look at me the way she used to. And when she turned and walked away without even a little kiss on the cheek, I wished that Grey hadn't bucked and sent me flying through the air. I wished that she'd taken off like a jet plane and taken me all the way to...

Tír na nÓg.

THEY SAID I WASN'T sick enough to stay in St Luke's but I wasn't well enough to go home.

'What will we do with him?' said the matron, her hands going up and down like the planks of a see-saw.

'There's only one place for him,' said the chief doctor. 'St Mary's.'

No, no, no.

Grey granite bricks, black wooden door, green clock tower.

Iron bars on the windows.

A blast of heat and bleach would hit ya in the face when ya stepped through the door and put your foot on a floor as shiny and as slippery as a river eel. And once you were in, there was no way out.

THERE WERE NINE other men in St Joseph's ward, all wearing beige.

Too, too many in one cage.

All lying in little beds covered with hairy blankets that scratched like hell and smelt like damp sheep in the middle of winter. I was always too warm during the day and too cold at night. And every night, once the lights went out, there was loads of grunting and groaning and creaking of bed springs. I used to imagine the creaks were the sound of the swing blowing in the wind in our orchard, the one I had made for my son for his fourth birthday.

But it wasn't all bad. After a few weeks I got used to it and the tablets they gave me made the headaches go away, until one day I didn't feel the urge to bang my head against a stone wall.

And the *cága* went away too.

No, no, no.
You won't get rid of us that easily.

I didn't mind taking those tablets even if they made my shoulders droop and I started to drag my feet around behind me like all the other bucks. I still took those tablets 'cos they made the pictures in my head of home all fuzzy and I wasn't sad anymore 'cos I couldn't rightly remember all that I'd lost. I still took those tablets even when they gave me funny dreams 'cos funny dreams are better than sad ones.

Haw, haw, haw.

WILD HORSES DRAG me from my bed and shove me down velvet cushion steps. I land on a floor that feels like grass, it's blue and smells of candyfloss. Mr Sun sits on a hill, he wears a smiley face. I blink in the white light and shut my eyes, they open again, overhead are pink marshmallow clouds. Jelly babies play hide and seek in nearby trees, a purple one wobbles over and tugs my arm. I grab his neck to choke him. My hands turn into Cola Bottles dusted with sugar. The purple baby licks them. My body shakes.

Thump.

I fall out of my bed.

The *cága* crowd around and laugh.

That was you when you were two.

HARRIET BROUGHT A cake that she got in a shop, I knew that 'cos the mushy part in the centre didn't taste like the cream that comes from cow's milk. It was too sticky and sweet. Still I ate a slice after I blew out the four candles. We sat in the dayroom, just me and her, and a *cág* perched on her head.

Lá breithe shona duit.
Happy birthday, Matt.

Nurse brought us two plates and forks and mugs of tea, even though it was only an hour before dinner and not the right time of the day to be having mugs of tea at all. Harriet fidgeted and looked at her watch the whole time she was there.

'It's hard to believe he's forty,' said the nurse, as she cut the cake.

'It is indeed,' said Harriet.

There were no children or adult voices singing 'Happy Birthday'.

~~THE BEST DAY EVER in that hospital was when we went to the sea-side.~~ The best day ever was the day Mr T started working in the hospital. The second best day was when he told the nurses to bring us on a day out.

> *We do love to be beside the sea-side.*
> *Lots of wriggly worms in the wet sand.*

'The sea air will do them the world of good,' said Mr T.

We mumbled and tumbled out of the mini-bus.

'Stay together,' Nurse shouted.

Waves crashed, dogs barked, a child as small as Eoin Paul was when he died squealed and followed her Mammy into the green-grey sea and she didn't see the jellyfish or slimy seaweed. I sniffed salt air and my grotty shoes. Then I sat on the damp sand, shook my salt and pepper head and closed my eyes and all sorts of words cluttered my brain.

Is the seaweed worried about how it drapes itself over a rock? Does rock want to go to the doctor for tablets to get rid of those ugly limpets on its face? Do the mussels in the crevices think about how to make themselves invisible so huge human hands won't pull them from their homes and plunge them into pots of boiling water?

I didn't like the smell of seaweed, it was worse than the green floors in the hospital or the piss soaked sheets on Jimmy's bed or the carbolic soap on the orderly's hands. I have a powerful nose; sometimes the pictures of my life fade and corners curl but never the smells.

> *What about our smell?*
> *You like that too, don't you?*

Mammy's perfume, Daddy's aftershave hiding his sour breath. Eoin Paul's skin after our Saturday night bath. Harriet's sweat after sex. Daughter's hands after eating ice-cream. Son's hair after a swim.

THE DAY I TURNED fifty, as soon as I was dressed and had my breakfast eaten I snuck into the dayroom, even though we weren't supposed to go there until eleven o'clock, and I waited and I waited.

Lá breithe shona duit.

When the dinner bell rang, I shuffled to the dining room, gobbled my dinner and scurried back to the dayroom again and I waited. Every time the big black front door's bell sounded, I jumped out of my chair. But it was never Harriet. And I waited. I tried my very best not to cry, didn't want the other men laughing. Though I knew some of them wouldn't even notice. When the nurse came to lock the dayroom before tea, I traipsed after her to the dining room, chewed on a ham sandwich, stared at the table and gulped my black tea. Then someone plonked a bun with a candle on top under my nose.

'Happy Birthday, Matt,' said Mr T.

'You remembered.'

'I remember all my patients' birthdays,' he said, in a voice that sounded just like Mammy's.

THEN THE WARD started to shrink. The older men stopped breathing, and when I'd try to wake them, their hands were so cold they'd nearly freeze mine too. And no new bucks replaced them. We were fewer and fewer until one day, Mr T said, 'Time for you to go, Matt.'

I sat on the edge of my bed looking down at my dull black shoes and said, 'Go where?'

To the lake, Matt.
Ar nós na gaoithe.

Now Again

THEY'VE PUT ME IN a house that I'm supposed to call home. In the middle of a huge estate, in my own tiny room, grey striped curtains on the window, blue duvet with white spots on the bed.

> *Too cold to sleep on, every third Wednesday.*
> *Another geis broken.*

No cracks in the ceiling, no other men snoring, no other beds creaking. Too quiet and not at all as warm as the ward in St Mary's. Some days I have to jump up and down to keep myself from freezing and that annoys the carers.

> *Silly billies.*

So they let me out to walk the town, all day, every day.

'As long as you're back in time for tea,' the woman of the house says.

> *Yucky beans on toast.*
> *Let's go to the lake*
> *and snack on juicy worms instead.*

'Exercise is good for you,' she says.

I WALK AND WALK around the ring road and the four roundabouts, then up and down Main Street and around Market Square. Sometimes I lie on the grass in the Mall and the school kids laugh at me and their parents pretend not to hear. Sometimes I go to the lake and watch the swans who I imagine are the children of Lir.

Who are we the children of Matt?

I listen to the distant roar of cars, trucks and lorries and breathe in nature's smells from montbretia, purple fireweed and forests of reeds.

You're gone awful poetic, in your old age.

I nod to St Patrick's mountain. It blows a breeze that wrinkles the lake's face.

DID YOU KNOW, they're not giving me as much tablets as they used to? Mr T says I don't need as much anymore. That they were giving me too many anyways.

Hip, hip, hurrah.
Now we can really play.

NOT ALL OF ME is daft, you see. Mr T never calls me that. It's just the part that hears the *cága*.

> *We'll keep you safe, Matt.*
> *Haven't we always?*

What do the *cága* see in me? Where are they really dragging me? Do they want to take the daft out of me?

Throw the D and f into the lake? Leave me with the M and a's and t's – M aa ttt.

> *Yes, Matt, yes.*

WHAT WOULD I be without the D and f? I'd be the man who made his wife a surprise dinner on her thirtieth birthday and didn't burn the steak. I'd be the man who showed his son how to hit a sliotar with a hurley stick. I'd be the man who helped his daughter make daisy necklaces in the meadow. I'd be the man who kissed his Mammy every night before going to bed. I'd be the man who ... had a brother who ...

> *But you're not that man, Matt.*
> *And if truth be told, you never were.*

Mr T's Notes About Me

Patient █████████

Name: █████████ Mullahy

DOB: 21st █████ 1945

Home Address: The Windy Gap, █████████,
Ballina, Co. Mayo

Next of Kin: ███████████ ██████ ████
Mullahy (daughter) ██████ Mullahy (son)

Occupation: Farmer

Date of Admission: ████ September, 1973

Diagnosis: ██████ trauma due to fall

Treatments: ████████ shock therapy, talk therapy,
medication ████████ mg

Date of Discharge: 13th March, 2005

Discharged by: Dr T█████████

Current residence: 223, Main █████████████

████████████████████

Current medication: ████ 250 mg twice daily

Prognosis: capable of ██████████ living

MR T HAS SHELVES and shelves of books in his musty office. Sometimes letters jump out of the books and I watch them float in the air, sometimes they make no sense and sometimes they do:

Interpretation of Dreams

Modern Man in Search of a Soul

Love's Executioner

A Way of Being

Man's Search for Meaning

Dark Nights of the Soul

Trauma and Recovery

Why Do Bad Things Happen to Good People?

'WHY DO BAD THINGS happen to good people, Mr T?'

He turns in his swivel chair and looks out the window. The gardener is mowing the grass and the lawnmower is making an awful racket. I try to pronounce the name of the man on the spine of one of the books but can't. So I cough to get Mr T to turn and look at me and when he does I point to the shelf.

'Do any of those books have the answer?' I ask.

'I wish they did,' says Mr T.

I start to sing the tune of my favourite TV show. He smiles.

'I wish you were part of the A-team,' I say. 'Then you could fix all the broken parts of me.'

> *Hee, hee, hee.*
> *Mr T in A-team is afraid of flying*
> *ain't gonna gettin' on no airplane.*
> *Oisín's big white horse isn't afraid of flying.*

BOOKS THAT USED to be on Mammy's shelf:

The Bible

Farmers Journal Country Cookbook

Better Homes New Cookbook

Ireland's Own Annual

The Complete Book of Knitting

The Adventures of the Fianna

Guess which one Eoin Paul and me liked the most?

Guess which one I threw into Eoin Paul's coffin when no one was looking?

I WENT TO SEE Mr T yesterday. He smelt nice. Like a mix of lemon and parsley. I asked him if he'd had fish for dinner. He smiled and said no but that his wife bought him a new aftershave for his birthday.

'One that both men and women can wear so I think she really bought it for herself, but that's our secret Matt. No need to tell anyone else that.'

You're good at keeping secrets, aren't you, Matt?

'OK,' I said.

'Do you like your new home?' he asked.

Harriet used to buy me aftershave for Christmas. I hated the smell of it, made me want to gag, but I wore it anyway.

'I like having my own room,' I said.

'Do you ever think about your farmhouse?'

'Nobody lives there anymore.'

Tell him to go away.

I wondered if this was some sort of test. He must have been able to read my mind 'cos then he said that I wouldn't be going back into the hospital again. I wasn't in that category of patients now. I wondered what category I was in, but I didn't ask him.

'You are not just a man with a hump. You are more than that,' he said.

The *cága* prodded me in the back. I jumped and raised my hands in the air.

Flap, flap, flap.

Mr T leaned back in his chair.

'I've lost all the *mores*,' I said.

I'VE LOST THE Daddy that might have shown his son how to shave and that might have walked his daughter down the aisle. The husband that might have brought his wife on a fancy holiday for their twenty-fifth wedding anniversary and the Granddad that might have wheeled his grandson around and around the garden in the wheelbarrow.

I could feel my face getting red and my hands were all sweaty. I ran to his desk, leaned towards him. Big bold letters jumped off his notebook, dangled like dead flies in a cobweb, I tried to make sense of them.

IN-STI-TU-TION-AL-ISED

What does that mean?

> *You're daft, Matt,*
> *daft, daft, daft.*

Don't keep saying that.

Mr T told me to sit down and he'd explain.

He went on a bit long and I was getting a fierce headache listening to him. I closed my eyes for a small while and then he stopped talking and the only sound that filled the room was the tick-tock of his big clock.

'So, I'm a lamb in a herd of goats, that acts the goat 'cos I don't know any better?'

Mr T smiles at me as if maybe I've finally made sense of something.

'I could go and live on my farm instead of being cooped up in a pen with all the other goats. And I'd be with Harriet again.'

'Harriet doesn't live there anymore,' he said. 'She's in a care home. She's forgotten who she is.'

How could you forget who you are? Bad and all as I am, I've never fully forgotten who I am or who she is or who my son and daughter are. I'd never forget.

Are you sure about that, Matt?

'You know the farm and house are still in your name,' said Mr T. 'Your daughter has leased the land but there's nobody living in the house.'

'Still in my name?'

'It can't be sold without your approval.'

'So this is a test then,' I said.

'I'm on your side, Matt.'

They don't let lunatics go home alone.

ONE DAY LAST week, I found a phone with a wire and I tried to call my son but I didn't have his number. I spoke into the phone anyway 'cos maybe just maybe he might hear my words.

Son, remember me, when you were three, hair as black as the saddle on your rocking horse, my voice as deep as your Action Man, my bucket hands scooped you up like a bulldozer. You shouted, 'Giddy-up horsey,' and tapped my broad back.

Remember, Good Friday when we caught an eel in the River Moy, your Mammy gutted it, threw it on the frying pan, the eel twisted and turned in melted goose grease and the three of us danced 'Ring a Ring o' Rosie' around the kitchen until the eel stopped twisting. Shouting and laughing, we raised the rooftops the day soldiers nailed Christ to the cross.

What do you see now in the opal mines of Coober Pedy? How can you stand the heat? Who puts you to bed in your underground home? Is there anything left of the used-to-be-me in your head?

HARRIET PHONED me last night and she asked when was I going to see her. Her voice sounded old and weary like the branch of a beech creaking in the wind, not at all like the voice I remembered.

'Shur, I'm talking to you now,' I said.

'This is dream talk,' she said, 'I want real talk.'

Close your ears, Matt.

She's hounding me in my sleep.

Wake up, Matt.

Every night hounding.

She left you
and now she wants you to go save her.
Silly, silly woman.

SOMETIMES I DO get tired of walking the ring road around town and all the busy roundabouts so I go on little train journeys to pass the time. I hop onto a carriage in Castlebar today.

> *There's only one place to go*
> *to escape your head,*
> *and the train can't bring you there.*

'Hi,' I say to the woman sitting opposite me.

She has as many creases on her face as I have on mine.

'I'm Matt and this is my hundredth time on the train.'

She looks at me, with a smile like a half-moon, then pulls out her phone.

My tummy rumbles from the click-clack sound the wheels are making on the tracks. I clutch my train pass.

'When will the man come to check the tickets?'

She looks at me the way Mammy used to when she'd be listening to the news on the radio and I'd be looking for a slice of her fruit cake.

'Not 'til we get to Athlone,' she says. Then she puts her phone back in her shiny red handbag, leans towards the window and closes her eyes.

Cliicckk, claacckk, chlicckk, claacckk.

'I'm only going as far as Claremorris. Have to be back in the house for tea. House rule – be home by six.'

She doesn't open her eyes. I turn away and press my nose flat against the window. All I can see is a blurrrrrrrrrrrr of greeeeeeeeeen. I wish I was going as far as Athlone. I wish I was going even further. All the way to Dublin.

All the way to Heaven.
That's where wishes come true.

I wish.

'Be careful what you wish for,' that's what Mam used to say when Eoin Paul and me'd blow all the seeds off a dandelion head and make secret wishes. But maybe today is the day I get my wish 'cos I'm not just going as far as Claremorris on the train.

It roars into Heuston. Last stop. Please mind the gap. *Seachain an bhearna le do thoil.*

Doors whoosh open. Footsteps on the platform, lots of footsteps. My hands shake, my neck's wet, my head jerks to and fro. 'Help!' I want to shout.

A big man in a hi-vis vest, chest like a pigeon, looks at my ticket and points me to a gate. I sit on a bench. Tap on my shoulder.

'Daddy.'

I spin around. Close my mouth, open it again, hope the right words will come out.

'Train back to Westport is at 6.15pm,' I say. My voice all wobbly.

She points to a restaurant called The Galway Hooker at the other end of the platform. When we go in I get the daily roast special. She has a coffee and watches me eat.

'You used to have such big hands,' she says.

I drop my knife and fork and look at them. Then gulp my pint glass of iced water.

'I wish I still had big hands.'

Then I just look at her for the longest time. She turns her head towards the opened window. A double decker bus passes by outside. Are the people on the bus easier to look at than me?

Depends on who's doing the looking, Matt.

Probably.

But at least now I can look and look and look without feeling awkward at the grown-up face that was once my little daughter's.

'This is my first time in Dublin.'

She turns towards me.

'You're very brave, I didn't think they'd let you come on your own.'

I take a huge chunk out of a roast potato.

'This is my first time in this restaurant.'

She hands me a tissue.

'Mine too.'

I use the tissue to blow my nose. There's an awful smell of cabbage in the air, reminds of the hospital. But I don't say that.

'Your Mammy used to cook bacon and cabbage every Saturday.'

'For as long I can remember, Saturday was mince day,' she says. 'She was always late back from town, what with the shopping and then going to the hospital.'

'I always asked after you and your brother,' I say.

'She told us the hospital was no place for children, it'd give us nightmares.'

She looks away again saying that.

'Am I scary now?'

'God, no, Daddy, I suspect you never were.'

ANOTHER BUS PASSES by outside and farts and I start to cough and splutter from the fumes. Dublin is too dirty and smelly to live in. Farms are dirty too but as Mammy used to say that's clean dirt. What if Daughter asks me to go live with her?

Silly Matt, nobody wants a daft
Daddy or granddaddy.

She talks about her husband wanting to sell the small apartment they live in, not enough space for them and the twins, and how they can't afford any decent house in Dublin.

'There's a big house on the farm and no one living there,' I say.

'The rent for the land is paying Mammy's care home fees,' she says.

'They've let me out of hospital, I'm in a community home but Mr T, he's my doctor, he says I could go live on the farm and you can all come too.'

Nnnnoooooo.

I don't know where the idea came out of, maybe it was a *cág* who put the words in my mouth but it wasn't the worst words I ever uttered. She looks over and under me, anywhere but straight at me.

'Do you remember when you were four, I'd hold your hand and we'd dance the hokey pokey around the kitchen?'

'I don't remember much of life before your fall,' she says.

Then she gets out her purse and starts showing me photos of her twins and I get an awful shock. I see my son's eyes in the boy and her eyes in the girl. Out of nowhere big waterfalls whoosh out of my eyes and run down the sides of my face and won't stop. I wipe my face with the backs of my hands but it's no use. She hands me another tissue.

She doesn't like cry-babies.

'Mr T says the farm and the house are still in my name,' I say when I manage to stop crying. And I was a long time crying.

'Yes, it's still in your name,' she says.

Then before I know it a man's voice shouts out of a big black speaker on the wall.

'Westport train departing from Platform 8.'

She walks me to the gate, we say goodbye, awkward hug. I hop onto the train and something tells me this day will never come again.

Just you and us, Matt,
don't need anyone else.

WHEN I GET OFF the train in Castlebar, it's dark, somewhere a dog barks, there's a scratching in my ear, like the scurry of mouse feet across a flagstone floor.

'Where will I go now?'

Follow us.

A taxi horn blows, I jump as high as a March lamb and I nod until my neck aches.

No, No, No.

I walk the ring road but not the way that leads me to the house I'm supposed to call home. I walk until I run out of path, I walk on the strip of grass between the road and the deep mucky ditch. I walk until there's no white line in the middle of the road, until the road turns into a lane, until grass grows in the middle of the lane, until there's more holes than lane, until the lane turns into gravel, until a rusty iron gate stops me in my tracks. And then I look up. The moon is round and full and it floodlights the house.

Moony, moony night.

If I could draw what I see in front of me with a pencil it would be a rectangle with squares on its face, a roof of smaller rectangles slipping and sliding, a tumbling down chimney stack on top, no smoke.

There's clumps of grass in the gutters leaning against each other like drunken Fianna warriors. I climb the iron gate, walk through the yard, knock on the door, then try to push it open. It doesn't budge. So I squeeze myself through one of the broken glass squares.

Ouch!

DUST RISES LIKE an ash cloud when I land with a thump onto the kitchen floor. I press the switch beside the door. There's still a bulb hanging from the ceiling and just like magic it lights up.

'Welcome home, Matt,' I say.

I don't remember the kitchen ever being so cold. I shiver then I swing my arms back and forth to warm myself up. There's no bucket of turf beside the hearth and there's a bird's nest in the fire grate. Something screeches. Then flap, flap, flap. I duck before a house-wren scratches my face.

'Shoo,' I say, 'Shoo, shoo, shoo.'

> *Silly little birdy.*
> *Can't shoo us away.*

He flies out the window I've just squeezed through. The big oak table Harriet and me bought in Galway still stands in the middle of the kitchen. No chairs. Mammy's old dresser leans against the far wall like Mammy used to lean against the front door watching Eoin Paul and me play pretend Fianna with ash sticks in the yard before the measles killed him. There's no sign of the willow-pattern plates that used to live on the dresser's shelves, only taken from their perches for Christmas. The belly of the house groans ...

No, it's us.
Too many memories
popping up in your head,
making us dizzy.

... in hunger for a lamb stew or maybe a rhubarb tart. Lines and cracks criss-cross the ceiling and I can smell damp and mouse poo. There's huge cobwebs in every corner. I shout and their tiny lines shake, spiders fall and scurry away. I crawl under the table like I used to do when I was three, rock back and forth, reminds me of Mammy and me in her rocking chair.

Hush-a-bye baby, on the tree top ...
When the bough breaks ...

I DREAM THAT Eoin Paul and me are having a picnic beside the whitethorn tree in the middle of the fairy fort in the lower field. Eoin Paul runs around with a whiskey bottle of tea in one hand and a crab apple in the other. I lie face up on the grass, the heat of the sun on my skin. Then the tree bends, gathers us into its arms and we laugh as it flies away with us.

Caaww, caaww,
haaww, haaww.

Claws wake me, shake me this way and that, I jump, bump my head off the roof of the table. Then through the broken kitchen windowpane I see a star sneak across the sky until it hangs like a chandelier over the fairy fort. I race outside.

Let's go play in the cathairín.
Is maith linn na daoine beaga.

I open the lower field gate. Tramp through the grass, avoiding the cow-pats. They start to smell more like strawberries than shite the nearer I get to the fort. Claws tap on my hump.

Féach!

The whitethorn in the middle of the fort shakes. The bank of earth around it turns into a circle of silver light. The tree's white blossoms fall like snowflakes. Its trunk leans towards me and its branches beckon. I scramble up the bank and down the other side. Then I throw myself into the whitethorn's mossy arms.

> *When the bough breaks,*
> *the cradle will fall,*
> *down will come baby,*
> *cradle and all …*

That's where Mr T and his helpers find me. The next day.

WHEN THEY BRING me back to the house I'm supposed to call home there's no tea on the table, even though it's six o'clock. But there's a big square cake with white icing on top and blue letters.

HAPPY 60TH BIRTHDAY.

But only six candles for me to blow out.

'Make a wish, Matt.'

I close my eyes real tight, blow and make another wish.

> *Lá breithe shona duit.*
> *You're too old for wishes to come true.*

I LIE IN MY BED all day in a room, in a house in the middle of an estate, in the middle of a town, where the only wild animals that roam are night foxes dipping their noses into rubbish bins. And cocks never crow.

Caaawww.
You'll have to stay in bed next Tuesday
if a cock doesn't crow.

UNDER MY BED lies a Jacob's USA biscuit tin. Bourbon Creams. Custard Creams. Jammie Dodgers used to live inside.

Munch, munch, munch.

A student nurse put the tin at the end of my bed one Christmas Eve, said he was Santa, but I knew his beard and red coat were fake. I'm not that daft, you know. By the time the wren boys called on St Stephen's Day I'd gobbled all the biscuits but I kept the tin. If you looked inside it now what would you find? Bits and bobs like ...

A cág feather.
Eoin Paul's mousy-brown hair.

... an elastic band, fish-hook. Needle, for sewing not injecting. A train ticket, black and white photo of two boys with ash spears in their hands, two torn pieces of a polaroid photo, one piece with a man and the other with a woman lying on a beach in Bali. Two baby photos. A black crayon and colouring book.

My biscuit tin life.

EVEN THOUGH IT'S a Tuesday, and there's no cock crowing, I have to get out of bed. They're bringing me back to the hospital. Mr T wants to see me again.

'Have you given up, Matt?' he asks.

Yes, yes, yes.

I twist and turn in his big leather chair. He sits on his desk, knees crossed, looks down at me through the square glasses on his nose. Then he turns, looks out the window, I follow his stare, a big fat cloud that looks like a combine harvester cuts across the sky. We watch and watch, then a white tractor follows and then an old hay rick.

'What are we going to do with you?' he says, still staring out the window.

Silly man, silly question.
Níl a fhios aige.

'Níl a fhios agam,' I say.

'Speak in English, Matt, I don't understand.'

He'll do whatever we tell him to do.

ON FRIDAYS ONE of Mr T's helpers brings me swimming. I dive, dive, dive to the bottom of the deep blue pool. I remember when Eoin Paul and me dove to the bottom of the river. Dive, dive, dive. Hold my breath 1 2 3 4 5 ...

I stay at the bottom as long as I can. There's no one to call me daft down here. I feel my eyes bulge like a mad auld trout. I open my mouth and close it again, open and close, cough and splutter.

PIT PAT, THAT'S HOW the *cága* chat. Their black claws tap dance on the wooden floor. Too many tapping, chatting, calling me to go this way and that.

> *Let's go to the lake, Matt.*
> *Then to Tír na nÓg.*

A claw catches my ear. I just want to stay in bed all day.

> *Get up, Matt.*

I roll over, look at the bedroom wall. Another claw pulls the hair on the back of my head and raps my hump. How do I get to Tír na nÓg? Claw pulling my ear whispers.

> *Easy peasy, go up Main Street, c'mon follow us. Down to the traffic lights at the junction and straight on, dodge the potholes, jump over the wall onto the lake path. See that wasn't so hard. Now, jump.*

Wait. Tír na nÓg isn't in the lake.

> *No, it's not in the lake but see that spot under the bridge where the sun can't reach, there's a big white horse with wings there, when you*

jump you'll land right on top and it will whisk
you straight up to the clouds. Up, up, up,
higher than the highest clouds and that's where
you'll find Eoin Paul and your Mammy ...

Stop. What if Daddy's there too?

That would be hell.

I WANT TO PAUSE the claws of the *cága*, stop them dragging me this way and that, their natters, skitters, screeches, muddle my brain, as mucky now as the bed on the bottom of the lake where eels wait ready to gnaw the trunk of me. I lie on the grass, arms spread out like Christ on the cross, legs as wide as a prisoner on a torture table. I pull clumps of grass, throw them in the air, pull at my hair, wish I was a lion in a lair and I could roar the *cága* away. I twist and turn, jump, land on my knees and palms, cock my bum in the air, sway this way and that, gnash my teeth, snarl, wings flutter in the breeze. It's not the *cága*. A robin alights from the branch of a nearby tree. Children laugh in the distance and I crouch down low.

DaftMatt, they will still see you.

Leave me alone, give me a minute's peace.

Let's go to the lake.

AT THE LAKESHORE, a worm wriggles between my
fingers.

'Don't worry, I'm not going to eat you.'

Yummy worms.

I had five sausages for breakfast so there wouldn't be
any room for him in my tummy even if I could kill
him. He stops wriggling or maybe he stopped 'cos I
squeezed my fingers. The little thing has gone limp.
The lake growls like a pit-bull. Thunder rumbles
overhead, like a tank on a battlefield, my head feels
like it's going to be split by lightning. I look at the
angry sky, hope hail will shred my skin and I will
disintegrate like a tissue, my fibres blown away until
there is nothing left of me. And I won't have to jump.

I stare across the lake to the clump of birch trees on
the other side. They shake their branches and a gust
of wind strips them of their melon-yellow leaves. I
stare at the ground once more. The snort and stump
of what sounds like a horse makes me look up. A
grey mare stands on the glassy face of the lake. She
shakes her head.

Trup, trup a chapaillín.

The hail stops. The mare plods towards the bank until she's standing right in front of me and lowers her head. Her nose touches mine. There's a boy with straw hair sitting on her back, spear in one hand, shield in the other. I wonder where he's from.

Tír na nÓg.

Shhsh. Don't frighten him, or he'll fall and turn into an old man just like me and I don't want an old man for a brother. I want the boy that was Eoin Paul.

You'll only find him if you jump.

Seconds spinning,
minutes milling,
hours hulking,
days dancing,
nights nodding,
weeks waking,
months mulling,
seasons sulking,
years yawning,
decades aching.

And still I can't reach out and   touch.

Jump, Matt, jump.
Put a carraig in your pocket.

I'd swap all the *cága* in the world just to have one last
jump in the haystack with Eoin Paul.

I'M THROWING A load of letters in the air, and I really don't care where they will land or what letter will lie beside the other or what one will land under or on top of another. I'm looking up. Fuck the hump.

The letters zig zag, go this way and that. Yes Eoin Paul, I'm looking up and no it's not your birthday but I'm still looking up.

Zig, zip, zap, zag, zonk, ponk, plonk.

All the letters of my life hiss and hump.

Bump.

I'm looking up and I'm not giving up. Now they're dancing and prancing ...

Ag damhsa agus ag rince.

... like the deer the Fianna chase, they're falling and falling. Where will they land? What words will be born? What sentences will turn into snakes? What story will they make?

How

many

letters

are

left

in

my

life?

WE LOVED HIM.
We did.
Every bit of the boy.
Every bit of the man.
His over-cooked spaghetti brain.
His bramble-thick hair.
His Nephin hump.
His baby-man face.
His shovel hands.
His pitchfork fingers.
His weeping-willow trunk.
His sapling legs.
We loved him.
We did.
We did our best.
We did.
We promised his Maaww.
We did.
We'll look after him, we said.
We did.
But we couldn't undo his burnt brain
or make his spaghetti straight and hard again.
We just wanted him to find suaimhneas.
We did.
He did.

We had to give him back to his Maaww.
                              We did.
              Táimid go hiomlán faoi thoinn.

Shhsh.

The whole world's gone still.
The whole world's gone quiet.

                              Shhsh ...